www.pakkinsland.com

**Other Books by
Gary & Rhoda Shipman**

•

Pakkins' Land
Volume 1:
Paul's Adventure

Coming Soon

•

Pakkins' Land
Volume 3:
Forgotten Dreams

PAKKINS' LAND

Quest for Kings

Volume Two

Gary & Rhoda Shipman

Salinas, California

Quest for Kings
Volume Two

Story:
Gary & Rhoda Shipman

Art:
Gary Shipman

Edited:
James Pruett & Rhoda Shipman

Cover:
Design — **Rhoda Shipman** Illustration — **Gary Shipman**

Coloring:
Gary Shipman

Send Comments to:
**Pakkins Presents
Gary and Rhoda Shipman
P.O. Box 10503
Salinas, Ca 93912**

E-Mail:
Pakkins-Land @Worldnet.att.net

Web Address:
www.pakkinsland.com

THIS BOOK
IS DEDICATED TO OUR WONDERFUL MOTHER...
MARY THOMAS

IN LOVING MEMORY

PAKKINS' LAND Volume Two: Quest For Kings copyright © 2001 by Gary & Rhoda Shipman, Pakkins Presents P. O. Box 10503 Salinas Ca 93912 All rights reserved. No part of this book may be reproduced or utilized in any form, or by any means without written permission except in the case of reprints in the context of reviews. Any similarities to persons living or dead is purely coincidental.

ISBN: 0-9700241-2-6

Printed in the USA

Table of Contents:

Overview 7

Chapter One
Quest for Kings 10

Chapter Two
The Gathering 33

Chapter Three
The Captive 61

Chapter Four
...And a Little Child Shall Lead Them 81

Chapter Five
Forbidden City 103

Glossary 127

Special Thanks 128

OVERVIEW

of
The Story Thus Far:

Our hero, Paul, sets out one day to explore a piece of property owned by a recluse known as "Old Man Pakkins." Almost as soon as he arrives he find a trail of blood that leads him into a cave. Paul winds up getting lost, but manages to get out of the cave only to find himself in a fantastic new world called Pakkins' Land, where animals talk and nothing is quite what it appears.

Paul encounters a great, radiant Eagle that gives him a single feather, which glows with its own light, symbolizing the power of good over evil, which Paul will need it in this strange new world.

Shortly after arriving Paul meets up with an unusual, little Jackal named Gus, he proudly announces that he is a lion. Gus takes Paul to meet the leader of the animals, a bear who goes by the name Mr. Brambles. Due to the growing threats of Rahsha, the evil ruler of the eastern land, the decision is made, that Gus will try to return Paul to his home.

Under the command of Rahsha a huge Dark-Flyer (Pip) attacks the two of them just before reaching the cave that leads to Paul's home...Gus bravely lunges into the deadly clutches of the Dark-Flyer, allowing Paul a chance to escape.

Despite his bravery, Gus fails in returning Paul home.

Paul chooses rather, to stay and help Gus, he takes hold of the feather that was given to him by the Great Eagle. A blast from the feather strikes the Dark-Flyer with such force that it's sent reeling and frees Gus.

The Dark-Flyer responds with a blast of his own which puts Paul over the edge of a great cliff.

CHAPTER ONE

Quest for Kings

CHAPTER TWO

The Gathering

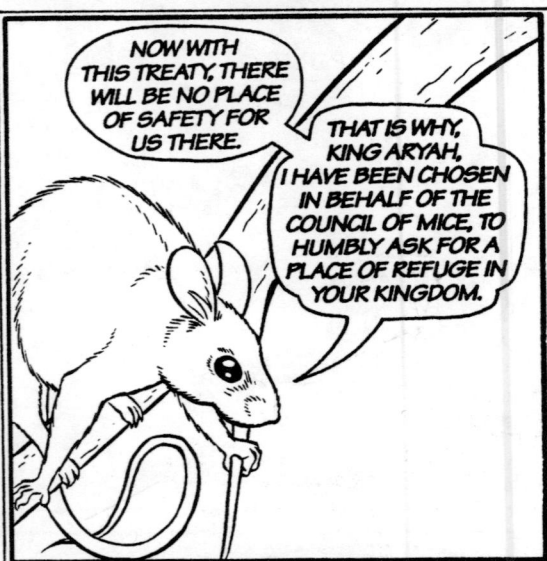

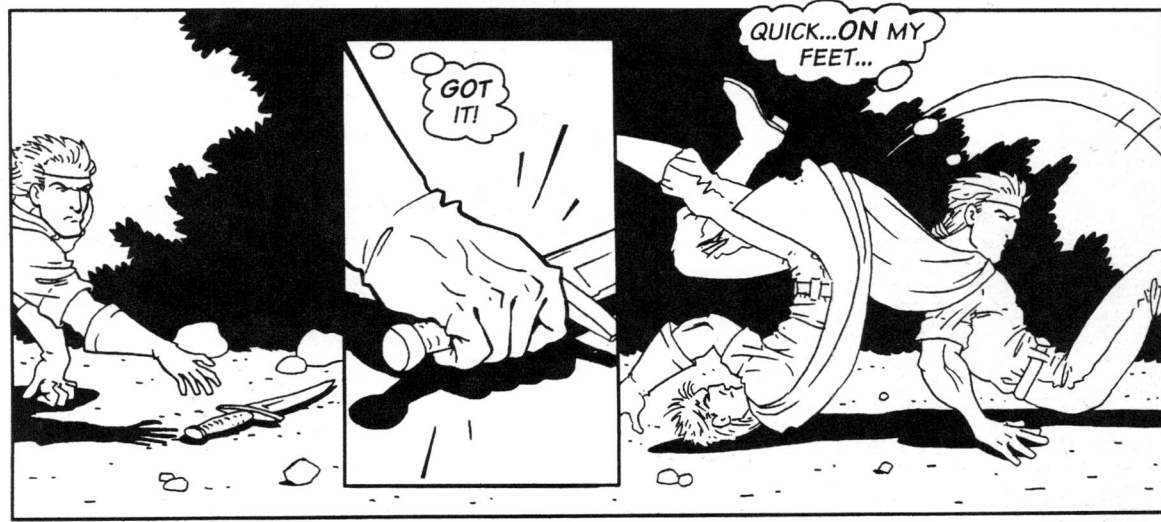

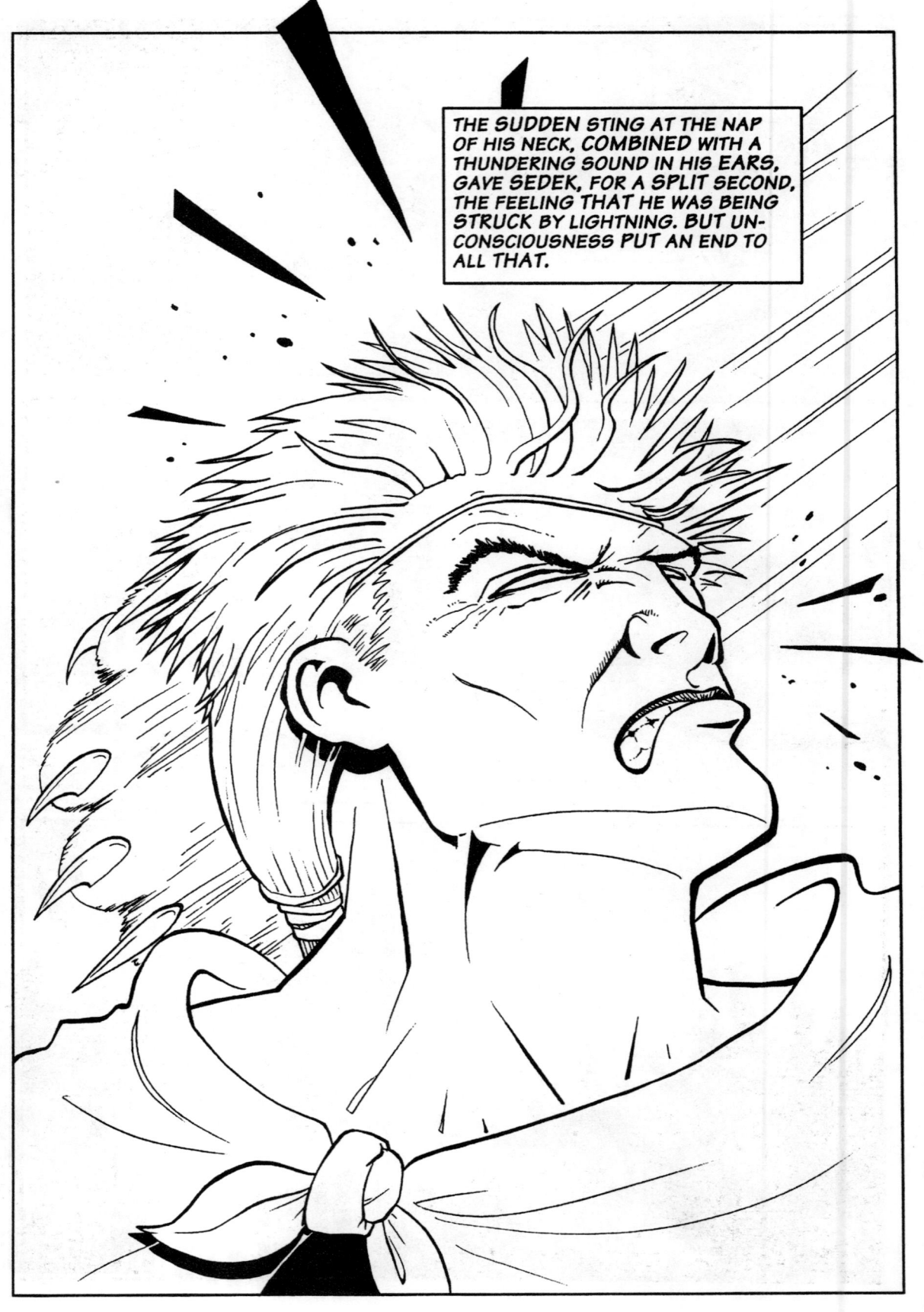

...AND NOISY JUNGLES.

WITH TIKVAH AND LILA GAINING ON THEM ALL THE WAY.

TIKVAH, LOOK! TRACKS!

YES! AND THEY SEEM LIKE MR. BRAMBLES'!

LET'S FOLLOW THEM.

man toting a sack full of body parts. Then nothing. I still hear breathing, but this time it is my own — or the sighing of the house, or the hot breath of the man upstairs, or the lungs of the corpse he has with him, collapsing gently.

On my way past the kitchen I hook my arm around the door and pick up a pot of blackberry jam, because a missile is safer than a knife. Halfway up the stairs I hear a wet rasping and sucking sound and the slap of something wet hitting a wall.

'Hello?' I say, because I am stupid that way.

Silence. The rasp-and-suck comes again. More silence. Whoever is, he is in my bedroom. I rest each leg on to each new [step] as if they were frost, cross the landing to my room and push open the door and look.

My bedroom wheels past; torn corner, ceiling, window sill, chair. My eyes are too [blind] to hear those [footsteps]. In any case, there is no-one there. Why didn't I hear those slow footsteps walking towards [me] across the empty room?

'Oh please.'

The footsteps have [stopped]. There is the same weeping noise. For a moment I think it comes from my own throat.

'Stephen stop it is that you?'

CHAPTER THREE

The Captive

---

drags him into the bathroom by the belt every time they have dinner with friends. Now he is talking about younger ass. I don't want to know. Married people should not tell tales. Being miserable in silence is the price they pay for being happy. They bought it. I did not. I am stuck with a couple of one-night-stands and an angel in the kitchen who breaks my appliances and won't put out. I understand the difference between sex and love, between love and the rest of your life. So don't let any married man tell me that he has problems with his dick. And keep their wives away from me too, at parties.

'An angel?' says Jo.

'Never mind,' I say.

'Hang on,' says Marcus. 'We were all virgins. Even you had a childhood and lost it. Or maybe you're born with a diaphragm installed, here in Dublin 4', and a little trail of insult crosses behind his eyes, like beads on a miserable string.

* * *

My mother thinks that the loss of my virginity caused my father's stroke and so do I. Never mind the facts. The first

THE HEAT OF THE DAY BEGAN SLOWLY TO WANE. THE GROUP OF US WHO HAD GATHERED ON THE BEACH MADE A FIRE TO KEEP THE COLD OF NIGHT AT BAY.

I HAD ONLY BEEN IN THIS STRANGE LAND FOR A SHORT TIME AND ALREADY I FELT A PEACE LIKE THAT OF HOME.

WE WERE IN THE FORBIDDEN EASTERN LANDS NOW.

NOT KNOWING THAT BY MORNING LIGHT WE WOULD BE SETTING OUT ON A QUEST THAT WOULD CHANGE US ALL.

MY COMPANIONS SAID IT WAS A DANGEROUS, UNFORGIVING PLACE.

MY THOUGHTS TOOK ME BACK TO THE BEGINNING, AND HOW IT HAD ALL BEGUN.

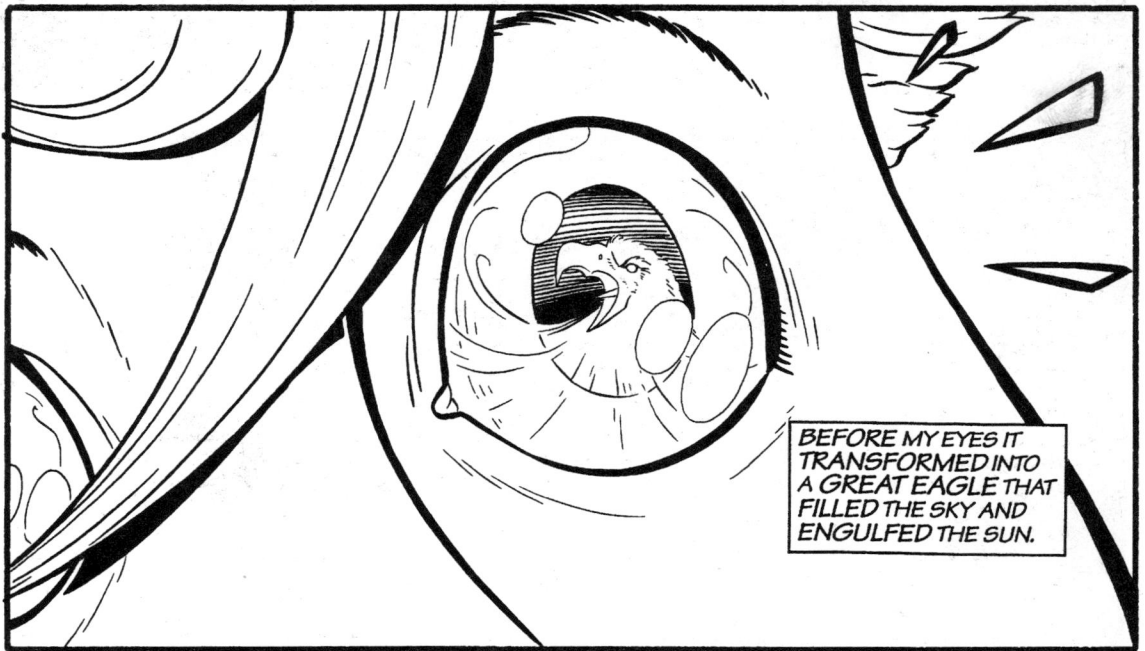

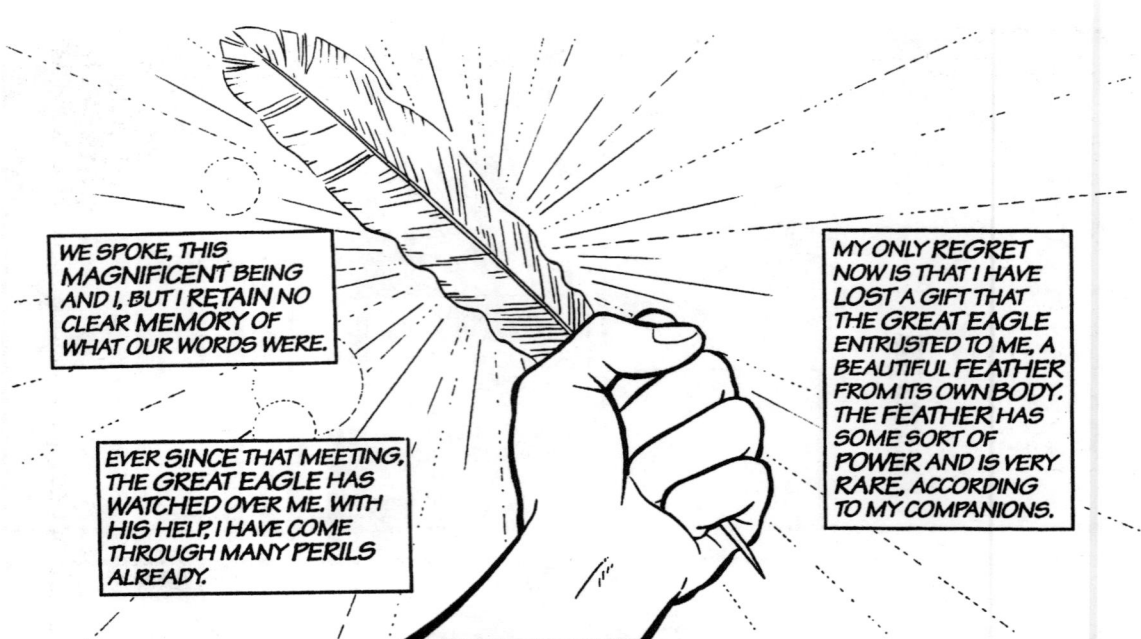

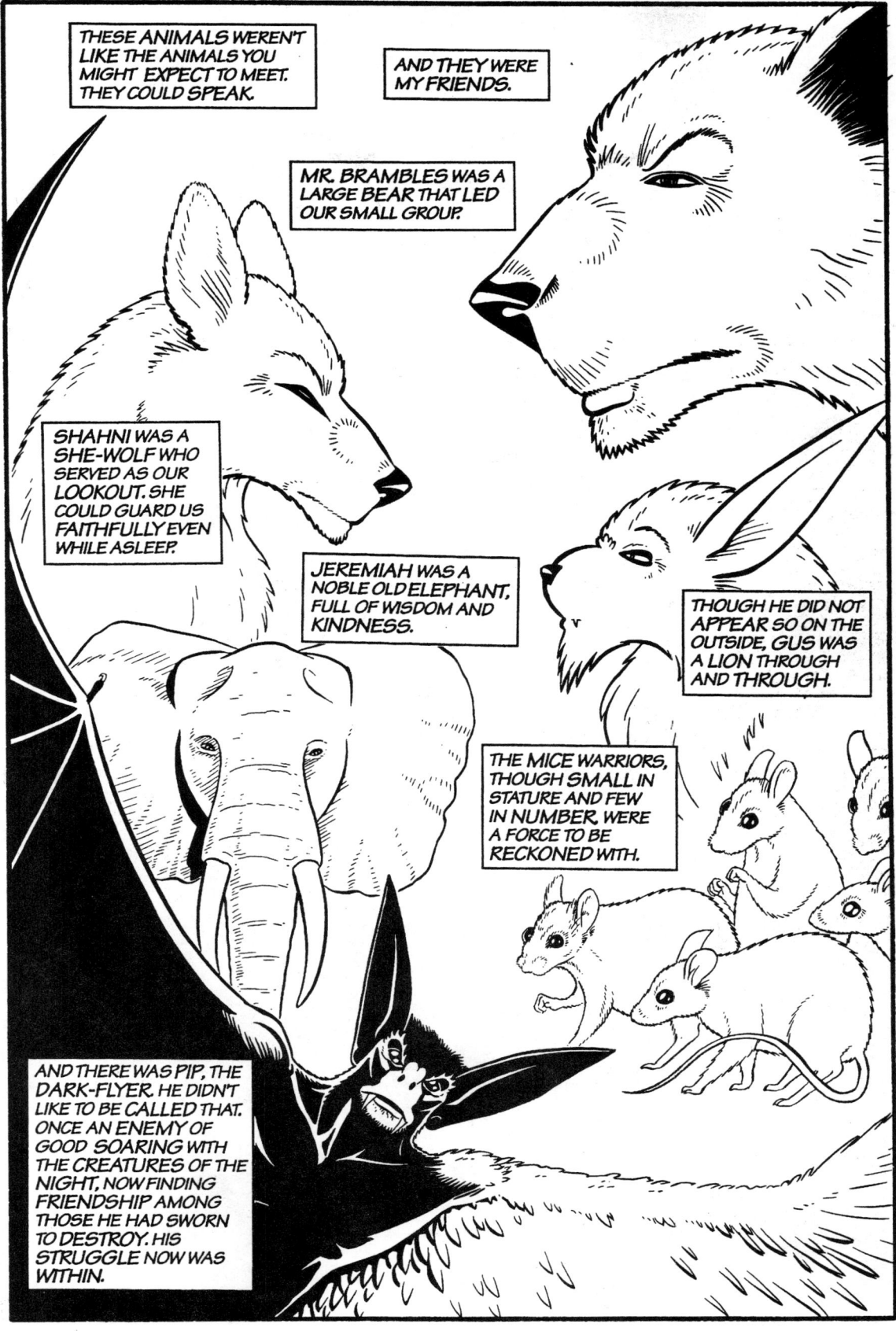

CHAPTER FOUR

...And a Little Child Shall Lead Them

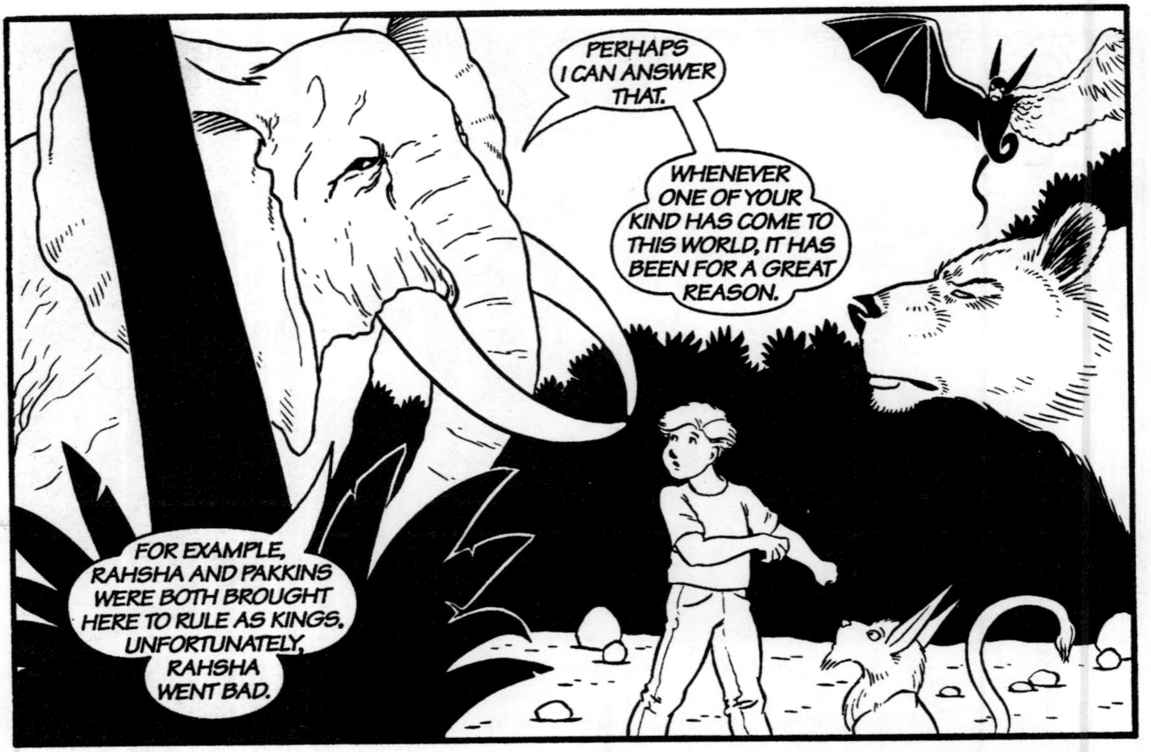

"PERHAPS I CAN ANSWER THAT."

"WHENEVER ONE OF YOUR KIND HAS COME TO THIS WORLD, IT HAS BEEN FOR A GREAT REASON."

"FOR EXAMPLE, RAHSHA AND PAKKINS WERE BOTH BROUGHT HERE TO RULE AS KINGS. UNFORTUNATELY, RAHSHA WENT BAD."

"RAHSHA KNOWS THAT IF A HUMAN COMES INTO THIS WORLD, HIS KINGDOM IS THREATENED."

"BUT I'M ONLY A BOY!"

"YES, A BOY WHO HAS SEEN THE GREAT EAGLE."

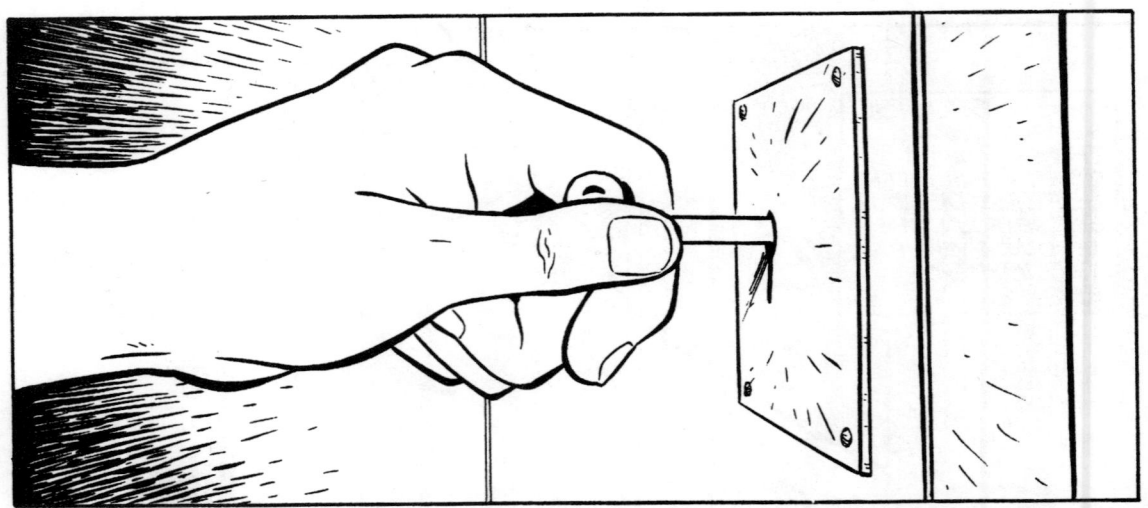

CHAPTER FIVE

Forbidden City

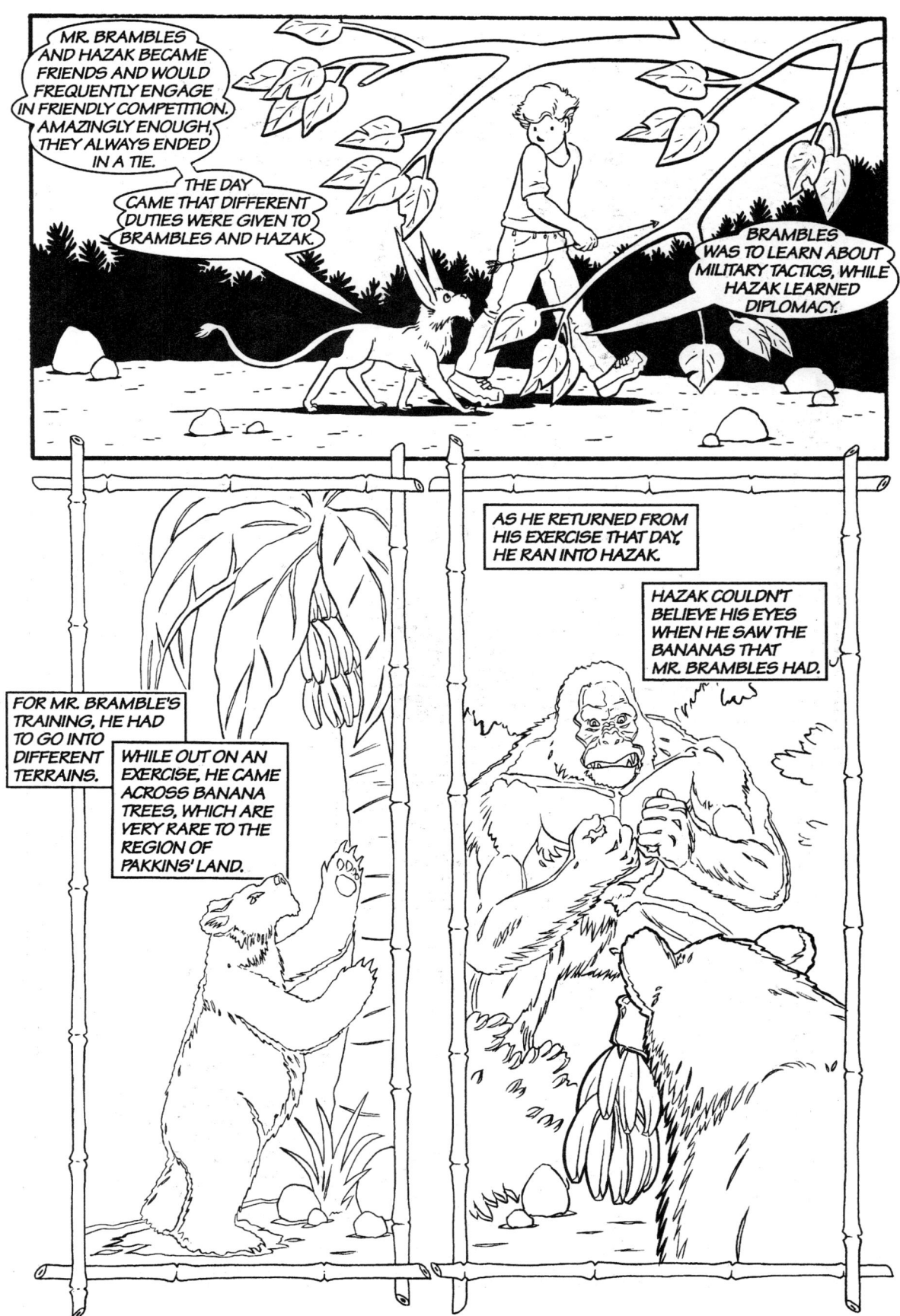

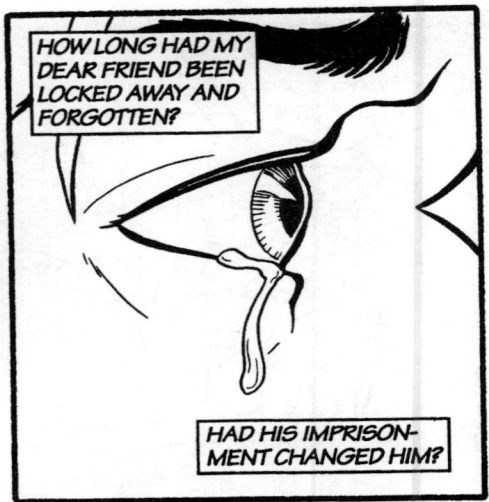

ALL RIGHT... LET'S GET MOVING, WE CAN'T AFFORD ANOTHER ENCOUNTER LIKE THAT.

MR. BRAMBLES, LOOK, THERE'S SOMETHING OVER THERE.

YES, THAT'S THE FORBIDDEN CITY.

Forgotten Dreams

GLOSSARY

Tikvah (Flying Squirrel) ....HOPE

Aryah (the King) ....LION

Rahsha (the Evil King) .... EVIL

Sedek (the King) .... RIGHTEOUSNESS

Hazak (the Gorilla) .... STRONG

Lila (the Racoon) ....NIGHT

Jeremiah (the Elephant) . THE LORD WILL RISE

Nahmer (the Tiger) .... LEOPARD

Samson (the Killer Whale).................... SUNLIGHT

OUR GRATITUDE
AND WARMEST THANKS
GOES TO

NATE BUTLER

JESSE HAMM

RICK LAW

GERRY AND TERRIE MCCONNELL
AND THE STAFF AT
MONTEREY COMPUTER CONSULTANT

RALPH MILLEY

VAN AND MARY PARTIBLE

AND

JIM PRUETT

WE ARE VERY GLAD TO HAVE HAD THE CHANCE
TO MEET ALL OF THESE WONDERFUL PEOPLE.
THEY HAVE BECOME DEAR FRIENDS.

ALL OF THE PRAYERS, AND SUPPORT WE HAVE
RECEIVED, ARE VERY MUCH APPRECIATED.